SANGAMITHTHIRAI SHORT STORIES

(POST COVID NOTICEABLE BEHAVIOR CHANGES WAVE-II)

J K PRADAP

Dedicated to

Doctors, Nurses, Police, Front line Administrators...ets, who had sacrificed their life for fight with Covid-19 multiple variant

Contents

Foreword

Few minutes

It is not a new attempt to express ten different points of view with one theme. But then, writing about current effects even as the problem persists was a hard feat. All the characters in this book are those who travel with me in this journey called life. I have just pointed out the variety of issues with these stories. I do not wish to detail further because it would all lean towards the medical line.

I am presenting these stories from a point of awareness. As I am not a doctor, I have avoided talking about a few issues. Where needed, I have expressed my views on Fire and Safety. As we all have a long journey ahead of us, let the concerned people write about their experiences after a lot of research. Though these problems could have been written as research papers, I have changed them into stories to ensure they reach a wider audience.

We cannot say with certainty that all this is due to the virus. But they are surely due to the situations and health effects created by that virus, I think. For example, this is like a bend in a new wheel. Even after straightening it, the wheel cannot function as before. But the human body would surely get its natural state back.

As I had also suffered from this situation and still feel the continued effects of these, I am providing these stories to you.

Thanks go to Ms. Dhivya Balaji, who translated these stories from Tamil to English on record time and Nikita, who edited these stories in English version.

You can share your thoughts to smiththirai@gmail.com

Shortly, I shall meet you with another book (novel).

J K Pradap

Acknowledgements

My love

To

Who making my life flow laminar

Sat

Laksmikanthan

Raj

Bala

Vinoth

Sridar

Thanks for their support and care

Manish

Durgesh

Priyanka

Sanjay

Ruchi

Saddam

Amar

Anjali

CHAPTER ONE

Yudhi

It was as he washed his face with water, wiped it with a towel, and wore his spectacles that he understood the truth. The moment he realised that even he had not escaped its clutches, he called his wife.

"Tell me... What's the matter?" asked Yudhi's wife.

"Listen to me clearly."

"What happened, dear?"

"Where are you now?"

"I am cooking."

"Is there anyone else near you?"

"No. Mother and Father have gone shopping. They are saying that there will be a lockdown in a couple of days."

"That's good. Just drop all the vessels in the sink and go to the room upstairs with all your dresses."

"What are you saying?"

"I think I have caught it too."

"But I came here two days ago..."

"It does not work like that. I am going to call the lab technician home for the test. You go upstairs. You may need to isolate for two weeks. Ask them to buy containers to parcel the food. Don't come outside for whatever reason. I will call you later."

"Oh my! In this state, I am not near you. You can't even cook!"

"I will arrange for food from a mess here. You first go upstairs."

"Okay, dear... My father and mother..."

"I will explain to them. You first take everything you need and isolate yourself." He disconnected the call and called his wife's father.

"Uncle, even Aunty and you should not roam outside. I am going to get myself tested. Don't go near anyone. Just go back home..."

"Son, what will you do?" his mother-in-law's voice rang out from behind.

"Aunty... I am a doctor. I will take care. You first go back home."

After the conversation, Yudhi sat on the bed and wondered what had to be done next. He called the university he worked in and requested his colleagues to get tested. He was thinking about anyone else who might have been close to him. No... No one else. As classes happened online mostly, there was no major issue. Nowadays, even his colleagues, the professors, did not come out of the cabin. Everything happened via mail at the university. People hesitated to even step out for tea and coffee. The peons were mandated to wear gloves and masks.

Even joining this lecturer's job was done for getting a government job by writing an exam for it, for which deeper and broader knowledge of the subject was required. Six months had passed in this job. He had worked as a physiotherapist in a hospital in the same town before. He never had the time to read back then. But now all types of books were easily available in the university's libraries. He spent more time than before reading. He applied for a government exam and was waiting for the exam date to be announced. And now he had contracted the virus.

Though he had gotten an invitation to work again for the hospital, he was hesitant to go back. In three months, the academic year would end. If he joined after that, there would be no issue with the current job, he assumed. Likewise, the problem was also becoming bigger.

Hearing the incoming message tone in his phone, he looked at it. The SMS informed him that the university was going to be closed starting the next, and online classes would continue until further notice. He thought that somehow the university management had come to know. Now everything else would go smoothly. Wanting to sort out the food first, he went to the kitchen and ensured the availability of all provisions including rice, lentils, oil, and vegetables. He thought that he could substitute milk with milk powder, or ask the vendor to leave the packets by the door. He did all the preparations for two-week quarantine. He took his mobile and updated the status on all social media sites— 'Corona positive. Don't disturb for a few days'. Moments after he updated the status, friends messaged him with advice or help. When it turned to a disturbance, he switched off the mobile. And since he was on the sixth floor, the chances for external contact were minimum.

That night, he took the batter from the fridge and made himself some *dosas*. As he ate, he realised that he had lost the sense of taste. After settling into bed, he wanted to call his wife and switched on his phone. A lot of messages had come. Eventually, when he called, she picked up immediately as if she had been waiting.

"Why have you switched off the phone?"

"It was disturbing, all the messages... Let that go... Were you able to taste your food?"

"Yes. Brinjal gravy. It tasted good."

"I seem to have lost my sense of taste. I will arrange for you to be tested tomorrow. Even if you don't have it, don't step out."

"Okay, dear. How are you feeling now?"

"It has not become severe so far. I will know by morning. Okay, you go to sleep. I will call you tomorrow. I'll switch off my phone now. If I don't call you by 8AM tomorrow, you call the intercom number."

"Okay."

"Good," he said, disconnected the call, and leaned back in his bed. Whirling in his thoughts for some time, he went to sleep.

In the morning, he heard the intercom blaring from the living room, and woke up. His body felt heavier, and his cough had increased.

"Hello."

"How are you?"

"Where are you calling from?"

"What is this? You were the one who said this last night... Have you forgotten?"

"Okay, wait..." he said and looked up at the wall clock. It was 08:30 in the morning. He remembered what he had told his wife last night.

"I feel weak. I just woke up."

"Then you go drink coffee first," she said and cut the call.

He found it hard to even lift the milk vessel. Not wanting to switch on the gas, he started the electric kettle, heated some water, and added the milk powder, sugar, and coffee powder. Then he poured it out into a glass and mixed it. Though he could not taste the coffee, he could taste the sweetness of the sugar. Even the smell was less intense. He decided that he no longer needed to test himself. He could go after four or five days. He would know the severity of this within a couple of days. Thinking that he'd know everything after that, he went and bathed.

It was only after finishing breakfast that he sensed his body temperature rising. His cough and headache increased. He called the doctor near his wife's place and arranged for them to test her.

Knowing that he had to be careful hereafter, he began analyzing his circadian rhythm.

Starting with his heartbeat, he started noticing the functioning of all his organs. Though his breathing was not obstructed yet, it was much weakened. Would he need an oxygen cylinder soon? Knowing the current situation, he prepared himself to face the crisis without needing oxygen cylinders. He asked the nearby mess to send him food for the afternoon. When there was no one around, he cleaned the door with a sanitizer, protecting himself with gloves and masks.

He called the apartment's security and informed him that the people from the other three flats on the sixth floor should avoid coming near his flat. He further requested the man to ring his doorbell every night to ensure he was alive and kicking. Then he advised that there was no need to spread unnecessary panic regarding the same.

Starting that evening, his health worsened. He developed breathing issues. He could not talk with anyone even over the phone so he switched it off and tried to sleep. But sleep eluded him and his body pained in extreme fatigue. He thought he could go to the balcony. But thinking it would create problems for those on the floors above and below him, if they happened to come out too, he opened the glass shutter and sat on a chair inside his house.

The evening sun soothed his skin. He would get his vitamin supply. That was when he noticed, on the roof of the school nearby, the pigeons were also sitting in the sun. He was not surprised. It was only humanity that was forgetting such wonders of the nature. Slowly raising his head, he noticed the mountains in the distance. Why did they seem farther away now? During the rainy season, the mountains would be full of lush green vegetation and seem much nearer. But now they were dry and far away. Everything was an illusion, after all. The distance would not have differed even by a centimeter. He roved his eyes over the surrounding landscape. It was dry everywhere. The summer had not yet reached its peak. When it did, the situation would worsen. The sun went down before he could ruminate further. He closed the shutter and went back inside. If he ate and went to bed soon, he could escape the fatigue. His doctor friends had offered to send him medicines, but he had denied asking them.

If he did not get some sleep that night, he could need further assistance. But the need never arose, and he slept well after dinner. But around midnight, his cough increased. He heated some water to drink, and it helped a bit. He was slightly afraid to even switch off the lights, so he went to bed with the lights on. But after some time, he realised that the night-times darkness was essential for enzyme regulation in his body and switched off the light. Tossing and turning, he felt his body going cold and then freezing. His brain was functioning but his body refused to cooperate. He was on his left side, and when he attempted to turn right, he felt that the upper side had become ice. When he tried harder, he felt out of breath.

His body started shaking and his blood flow stuttered. His fear increased and he wondered if he could yell out for someone. But his body triggered into action and the ice broke as his blood flow resumed. He flipped to his right as he calmed himself and realised that he had had a near-death experience.

Once again, he shook his body and felt the blood flow to all parts. If the virus affected such a young body to this extent, what would be the case for older people? He could not even imagine. His frozen body was giving him so much pain.

Since his body was younger, he could escape the clutches of the deadly disease. He would surely have died if that were not the case. He switched on the lights and reclined on his bed. He could feel the atrocities the virus was doing on his body. If he had not had normal breathing, he would surely have frozen to death. It was natural for this immunity to have gone down in the older people's bodies. Put another way, if the body lost its immunity at the last moment, it would definitely lead to death. This could happen to anybody. But a majority of the bodies in this world would have developed herd immunity. If that were triggered, the rates of death could be reduced.

The virus had not yet left his body. So, it still had the potential to give him more issues. But he would face it with courage. Choosing to recline instead of lying down, he closed his eyes. Despite the bright lamps, he slept well.

When he woke the next morning, he could sense some burning in his eyes. His temperature had also increased. He did not feel the usual morning freshness. He finished his morning ablutions and called his wife.

"The results of the test yesterday have come out positive, dear. But I do not feel any serious effects!" she said.

"I think it has not yet affected you badly. It is happening now, for me."

"What are you saying? How are you doing?"

"Let it go now. I will tell you later. Take your medicines properly. Call me if your temperature increases. I am not able to talk now. I will switch off the phone. Are Uncle and Aunty positive too?"

"We will know only tomorrow."

"Okay, I will call later," he said and cut the call. He reclined in his chair and switched on the TV. All the channels frightened him in the name of relaying the truth. So, he switched off the TV and decided to see something on his laptop instead.

But his concentration was being diverted. He could not bring his mind to focus like before. He sat silently, wanting to relax. But thoughts invaded his mind. He wrote down the details of all his bank accounts, passwords and other such important things in a diary, under that day's page. Though his wife knew all his secrets, he wrote some more things in that diary.

When he went to rest on the bed, he fell asleep. His body froze again like it had done that morning.

The torture continued for two days. All the taste went off his food. His circadian rhythm was thrown off. His body clock went awry. And in the midst of all that, he had gotten the disturbing news from his wife.

"I am having a bit of cough and a sore throat. I am only having a slight headache but I am feeling a glaring in my eyes, and that is frightening me. What if I lose my eyesight?"

"Nothing like that will happen. For one second in the eyes and two seconds in the ears, we will feel a recap of the most recent stimuli. Or we will not be able to continuously see and hear. How many seconds is it lasting for you?"

"About five seconds. Like they show in the movies, I am getting colorful flashes in front of my eyes. Even my brain is not working at that time. Won't our hands automatically go to rub our eyes? Even that is not happening. This is happening at least 4-5 times in a day."

"How many days has this been happening since?"

"About two days."

"If this continues today and tomorrow, go and get admitted to a hospital. I will ask around about this and tell you."

"How are you feeling?"

"I am better now. I am going to get tested in three days. I think it is lucky that this has not spread to Aunty and Uncle."

"Yes, dear. They are insisting on at least watching me from afar when I open the window. My mother's eyes tear up every time."

"Not just us...the entire world is reeling under this."

"Yes... Why are you switching off your phone often?"

"Nowadays, when I get phone calls while asleep, I get angry and end up being rude to the caller. And I regret it later. I don't understand why this is happening. I should check if this is happening even after I am cured."

"Okay dear... Let me not disturb you either..."

"You take your tablets and then some rest." He relapsed into his thoughts. The virus was attacking the body's organs based on which was weaker. How many organs would it affect like this? They would know the full details only a few years down the lane. Until then, mankind had to live with whatever light could be found in the complete darkness.

In just a few days, they were both cured and back to normal. But even then, he was still answering calls angry. So, he switched off his phone before going to sleep and made that a habit.

When that continued even during the daytime, he started facing many problems. He thought hard about how to overcome that. He had shown his rage against everyone but his mother. So, he called his mother one night and asked her to call in an hour. And he went to sleep without switching off his mobile. And exactly an hour later, his mother called him. He felt the anger. On hearing his mother's voice, however, he mellowed down and said in a pleading tone, "I am sleeping, Mom. I will talk later."

"You were the one who asked me to call!"

"When?" he asked, regaining consciousness.

"An hour ago," his mother said.

Realising the truth in that, he calmed down. He felt a renewed hope that this rage would clear soon.

CHAPTER TWO

Pooja

Sleep eluded her as Pooja tossed and turned in bed. Despite repeatedly closing and opening her eyes, trying to calm her mind, it did not look like sleep would pay a visit. She felt like she was being troubled by wide-awake, hyperactive children. She turned to look at her husband. He looked peacefully asleep. She remembered that he had tried to fall asleep by embracing her just a while ago. Why? She wondered. Why was she not able to match his vigour?

It had not even been a year since their marriage. Had she gotten frustrated with it already? But there was no such problem between them that warranted this. Even if something like that did happen, it did not have a great impact. She did love his teasing banter and cajoling. Oftentimes, she was immersed in his charm. And she had brought up playfights with him for that too.

She did not know how such feelings could have changed. Her love for him was the same, no less than before. But his mischief nowadays irritated her. Sometimes, it also angered her. She was confused. 'Why have I changed like this?'

Deciding that thinking over this was pointless, she rose and walked towards the kitchen. She drank a little water and realised that she wanted something warm for her throat. She switched on the gas, wanting to make herself some tea. She wondered if she should ask her husband if he needed a cup, too, and then remembered that he was sleeping.

With the teacup in hand, she stood on the balcony and sipped her tea, watching the school playground nearby. Within two sips, she felt the comforting warmth spread through her. She understood that if we give the body what it needs, our feelings will not trouble us. She sat on the cement bench and drank her tea. It was on this bench that she had sat with her husband many times in the past year and talked sweet nothings. How happy she had felt during those times! She would even feel proud of him. But nowadays, she consciously avoided sitting here with him. But there had been no such change in his behaviour. Why was she alone experiencing such a change in her mindset? Tears formed in her eyes at her heart's confusion. Was it because she was under the horrible torment of the virus for those twenty days? Even then, when he had hugged her, how safe she had felt!

It was a time when they had both isolated themselves in the house.

Her superiors at the office had allowed her the freedom to work only when she was able to. And true to that, she finished her work when it was convenient for her, sometimes even working at night. Even though some of the work stagnated, her office did not take her to task for that.

But her husband's job suffered. As he was employed in the marketing department of his company, a huge part of his work took a hit. It looked like he would get only half his salary. Unmindful of all that, they focused on getting their health back on track.

Hoping that doing yoga would increase their strength, they started practicing it. But because they could not do it properly, it only increased their weakness. Later, they got into a routine of walking and doing basic home workouts. When that had a good effect, they believed that they had gotten back to normal. There were no changes in her husband's activities but she realised that she had changed. Even though she wanted to share this with her mother and friends, her mind prevented her. And now, it had become a seriously worrisome problem.

She decided to approach her doctor friend the next day and get her advice. It was the same friend who, when they were isolating, had patiently explained over video calls how they could test themselves.

When she measured her temperature once, the reading was 93 F and she got worried. Wasn't one of the symptoms a high body temperature? But she was shocked that her temperature was much lower than average. But her doctor friend comforted her and explained that some people showed symptoms this way. She also gave some more health advice to follow. Within two days, as her body temperature returned to normal, Pooja felt relieved.

How the lingering fear had consumed her those days! But her husband had laughed it off, casually comforting her saying, 'This too shall pass!'

How close she had felt to him then! Why had that changed now? And how? She had many questions, but no answers. Would that be an aftereffect of the virus? With that uncertainty, she could not take a solid step.

Was the virus capable of causing such side effects? But she could not delve into that line of thought. Was all this happening only to her? Or were others facing such issues too? Until that point, she had no solid correlating data. Eventually deciding that only time would answer these questions, she went back into the house, tossed her teacup into the sink, and returned to the bedroom. Her sleeping husband had turned on his right now. She was overcome by the urge to lock herself in his warm embrace. The rainy season had begun, too. The habit of automatically searching for a blanket even in her sleep during the middle of the night had reared.

It was nearing midnight then. Initially wanting to reduce the speed of the ceiling fan, she then decided that it was more comfortable to lie on the bed. He would hug her close in his sleep shortly, she knew. She could close her eyes till then, if not able to fall asleep. Her thoughts continued to torment her, though.

Just a few more days! Then everything would be alright. If everyone took their vaccines properly, the effect of this virus could be reduced. But until then, she had to grit her teeth and bear all this. The solution to this was not in anyone's hands. Such calamities came rarely. One was happening right now!

There was a time when a bout of cholera severely decimated the human population. But it was eventually controlled. Every such disease would meet its end one day, and the world will return to normal. She felt the confidence giving her peace.

She opened her eyes and turned to look at her husband. Her feminine side took over, and she took his hands in hers, gently kissed them, muttering, "This too shall pass, darling husband. And until then, please bear with me!"

CHAPTER THREE

Siva

Siva guessed that the youngster was searching for something. Two days had passed since he came to the Covid ward. He was losing sleep, unable to bear the incessant coughing noises during the nights. But for Siva, who had been there for 6 days, this was not a big deal. But the youngster was able to sleep properly only closer to dawn.

He would wake up at 9 AM, brush his teeth, have his breakfast without bathing and then go back to sleep again. But the group of carrom players would begin their game and his sleep would be disturbed. Siva was noticing all this. He understood that the youngster needed something. It was clear from his activities though that he was not the type to approach anyone by himself. He had not spoken much to anyone since the last two days. His days were spent languishing with his mobile. It angered Siva to see him immersed in his mobile. Why? Why were people ruining their eyes, neck, and internal organs voluntarily? Why was humankind not yet fully aware of the horrors of not taking care of one's body?

"Brother, come here," Siva called the youngster, who was clearly hesitant to come closer. He just widened his eyes, as if asking, 'what?'

In response, Siva gestured and patted the bed next to him. The youngster pressed a button and came closer to Siva with the mobile in his hand.

"I am still covid positive. So, sit here," Siva invited him.

"Tell me. What's the matter?"

"Your name?"

"Sasi."

"Good name. I feel that you are looking for something. If you tell me, I could try to do it."

"Nothing like that!" the boy exclaimed, covering his mouth with his left palm. He rose, clearly indicating that he was not interested in talking further.

"Do you need a cigarette?" Siva asked directly.

Though there was shock on the youngster's face; there was also a flicker of yearning. Siva waited for him to answer.

"I am finding it tough, brother," the boy said by way of explaining his suffering.

"Then why are you alone? You can go and play carrom, chess or even cricket with them! Your mind will be diverted."

"Everyone is a stranger to me ..."

"Everyone is new indeed, brother. Even our sufferings due to the virus are new. So shall we leave everything be?"

Wanting to prolong the talk, Sasi sat there comfortably. Seeing his posture gave Siva the confidence that the conversation could continue.

"You tell me about yourself, and then I will tell you about myself," Siva offered.

Sasi looked up at him and began talking.

"I studied B. Com and I am working in the accounts department of a company. I hail from the nearby town. When they announced the lockdown, my father and mother took a car from our house and brought me back."

"Is your father working a government job?"

"Yeah. He is in the Revenue Department."

"How long have you been smoking?"

"About four years..."

"Have you tried stopping in between?"

"Yeah, I tried twice because a friend suggested I should. But I could not sustain for even two months. So then without her knowing..." He laughed, unable to complete the sentence.

"You cannot do that in this ward, brother. Even if you smoke in the bathroom, the smoke will come out and everyone will start coughing. Besides, even your oxygen levels will go down and create complications. You must surely know about the oxygen demand. Why, though? Your house must be big enough. You will probably have a room for yourself. Why have you not isolated at home?"

"My mother took care of me even after I tested positive and thus, contracted the virus herself too. My father was the one who assured me that he would take care of my mother and he sent me here."

"That is the best course for both of you," Siva said and observed Sasi closely.

Sasi, though, was immersed in some other thoughts. Siva relapsed into silence too, not wanting to disturb him. But in a few moments, as if he was just reminded, Sasi began, "You said you will tell me about yourself, brother..."

"Yeah, I will," Siva began. "My name is Sivanandam. My father is a devotee of Siva. He also knows a bit of tantric art. The village people come to us for things like a snake bite. I shed all that, studied B.Sc., Physics, and am working as a storekeeper. I tried thrice for a government job but missed landing one. Now I have crossed the age too."

"Are you not married?"

"There was a time when I believed it was a silly thing. My brother and I are two sons of the household. He followed all the rules laid out by society and lived a proper life. I was not interested in things like marriage though."

"Did you not love anyone?" Sasi asked.

Siva coughed out, laughing.

"Did I ask something wrong?"

"No, brother. Who can escape the clutches of love? I fell in love four times at different times in my life. Nature keeps giving you chances for such things. Some make use of it, some move away due to societal constraints."

"Did you not get a bride on your family's side?"

“There a lot of women there. But I do not think they will last.”

“I can’t understand...” Sasi replied, just as the lunch bell rang.

“Let us eat now, and then we can continue,” Siva said.

“You wait here... I will bring a cover for you,” Sasi said and moved towards the door.

Siva watched him go. Humans had only a little hesitation. Things became cordial soon, he mused. He washed both his and Sasi’s plates before the younger man returned.

“Oh, you have washed it! I will sit and have lunch with you here,” Sasi said, spreading an old newspaper on the bed. As they were eating, Sasi exclaimed, “All the items are good. I just cannot eat...”

“Apparently, we must eat 2500 calories a day. So, they are including a variety of items for that. Don’t waste any of it... Eat it all even if it takes time,” Siva said.

“I don’t think I can eat even half of it.”

“Distract yourself in conversation and eat slowly,”

“How many people are here in all?”

“There are 24 beds. I think there are more in the next room.”

“Looks like all the beds are full.”

“If we look at the situation outside, I think they will allot other rooms for those of us here who are a bit better.”

“Are you from this place?”

“No. I caught the virus when I returned from Bengaluru. I did not have any symptoms. Just a mild headache. But I came...” Siva responded, and focused on eating. He looked around and saw that everyone was eating their lunch. The older ones were a bit slow. Though their faces were pained, they still showed hope that they should escape this. Who does not like living? While fighting with such an invisible enemy, mankind naturally gets the fighting and survival instincts.

“Do you not get the urge to marry at least now?”

“When I see everything that is happening, I am torn between wanting to marry and also thinking that it would be better overall if I don’t marry.”

“Seeing your health condition, I am sure nothing will happen to you, brother,” Sasi said earnestly.

Siva accepted that with a smile. They took 30 minutes to finish their lunch.

They put the leftovers in a cover and deposited it in a separate dustbin. Then they washed their hands and returned to their room. The carrom gang had resumed playing.

“I am unable to sleep because of the noise of the carrom players. But how are the elders able to sleep?”

“They aren’t sleeping... They just do not want to disturb the younger ones and they are lying with their eyes closed,” Siva replied. They made six rounds of the ward and then Siva came towards his bed, saying, “You go to bed now. We will talk tonight.”

That night, after dinner, they both sat together on Siva’s bed and began talking. But noticing that many people were getting ready to sleep, they rose to go to a different place. Siva took their masks while Sasi brought out the bottle of sanitiser from his bag. The ward nurse objected to them stepping out. But the men explained that they were getting depressed from being cooped up and they would return in half an hour without causing any hindrance.

Another nurse instructed that while they had no permission to go via the front doors, they could go via the back doors but must return in ten minutes. She also added that they should not touch anything else. The men went to the back entrance and sat on the bench under the tree there. The lights of the city glowed in the distance. Bikes were busy plying on the main road even that late, and they could see the glowing headlights.

The men relaxed a bit and settled but they did not get the urge to talk. They appeared to have gone deep into their thoughts. Sasi began after a while.

“It would be great to smoke a cigarette now,”

Siva looked up at him, gently patted his shoulder and turned towards him as if he had a lot to discuss.

“If your yearning were right, you would surely have gotten it by now,”

"I am not able to understand..."

"If I had yearned for drinks by now, I would certainly have gotten them much earlier."

"How so?"

"Even I cannot understand that. I wonder if it is in my genes. I am taking drinks at night for the last ten years. But I have never gone to bed even once without drinks. Even if I stayed in the dry states."

"Maybe some people just are lucky that way."

"I have not put in many efforts, though. Initially, I began drinking with friends. And then, when I lived alone on the pretext of work, I started drinking alone. At first, I had no problems, my heart grew lighter. I was stressed from what I thought was an unworthy job. I started to hurt others under the influence of alcohol. I crossed my limits in a few days. I became a different person during the nights and in the mornings, I would regret it. My entire lifestyle changed. I slowly began to live an isolated life."

"You look like a good person. How did this happen?"

"That is the truth, brother. Maybe our friends and family would tolerate it. But the women who worked with me? I started advising them as if, I was the only righteous human. That too under the influence of alcohol in the nights. It made women away from me. It looked like there was no big loss. But I realised later that I had intruded into their privacy. But what could I do? Hindsight is stronger."

"What would you do? To regret like this?"

"Alcohol... creates a lot of issues for different people. For me, I started taking note of the people around me and became an odd person. Initially, I started telling my friends what I thought of them. It was ninety percent right. Bolstered by that and under the effect of alcohol, I could understand people's mindsets. Automatically, I could clearly understand if it would be a problematic day. It is an art. And somehow I got it. I would not give the credit for this to alcohol, though."

"Oh, so that's why you first approached me."

"That's nothing, brother. It is natural. But see... the virus did not attack me while I was regularly drinking. Right when I stopped drinking and started regularly jogging in the mornings to reduce my stomach, I got affected. I am laughing at myself. Maybe what people say would come true!"

"Yeah... even some of my friends are thinking that and drinking," Sasi added.

Siva laughed out loud, and then stopped himself, remembering the situation.

"Let that be, brother. How is this covid affecting your body?"

"My body feels heavy at times. I am not feeling hungry at all but I feel as if some people are sitting on my body and pummeling it. My headaches are bad. But I have no breathing difficulties."

"We are two kilometers away from the city. The air is better here."

"Many times, I would feel something pressing on me in my sleep. My stomach is stone-heavy and I feel pain during coughing."

"I do not have it that bad. I feel a bit exhausted. But understand one thing. Now we have a good chance of surviving but if something like radiation had affected this world nothing could have saved us."

"You are right, brother. But a lot of people have died!"

"This pandemic has completely shaken the world. The effects would not be visible now. Maybe ten years down the line we could see the issues. A lot of families have uncertain futures... I feel really worried to think of all that," Siva trailed off.

Sasi sat silently worrying about the future too. The covid pandemic had made a joke out of even education. All the rules known to mankind were being rewritten. The truth was that no one could oppose this.

This thing was affecting multiple generations. The smartest brains around the world were still trying to gauge the effects. But we would understand it only by living through it.

"Okay, come let's go back." Siva rose, and the men walked towards their ward. Despite them walking without a small noise, the nurse, who was half asleep, woke up and went back to sleep without saying a word to them. The men heaved a sigh of relief.

They spent a lot of their time like that, in conversation. First Siva tested negative and he took leave of his ward mates. Unwilling to return to work, he spent two days at home, in peace. He did not even get the urge to drink in the evenings, he noted with surprise. On the third day, he returned to the company and began working. Not much had changed. As transportation and logistics were affected at that time, the stock inflow was less.

The company was working a half roster, that too only those who were strictly needed.

In the evenings, when he crossed the wine shop on his way back, he did not get any kind of interest in the drink. His health returned to normal many days later.

One evening, when returning, he wanted to celebrate that day because nights always want to get celebrated. He went inside the shop and the shopkeeper smiled at him in welcome. Siva nodded to him, got himself a full bottle, and came back to his bike. Just as he was trying to set the bottle in the pocket of the cover on the petrol tank, it slipped from his hands and shattered at his feet.

Siva stood stunned for a moment. Then, in his head, he began laughing. A short distance away, a woman colleague of his laughed at his plight. Siva felt blushed.

He understood that now onwards alcohol was not the elixir of nightly celebrations.

CHAPTER FOUR

Oviya

Nandhini was sitting on the chair, watching the silent beauty of Oviya, who was sleeping on the cot. A small prick of guilt touched her heart on knowing that the virus had spread to Oviya from her.

"Nandhu, don't be upset about this. It could have come from someone else too. It just came from you, that's all," she had said to console her.

Last week when Nandhini had visited the house four hours away, Oviya had known about that somehow. Oviya, on seeing the woman who had returned in the night suffering to open her eyes in the morning, said, "Just lie down. I will bring a wet towel."

And then she had started helping her. Since they were staying in a PG accommodation, Oviya closed the door immediately. Because both of them had always liked letting in the morning sun rays, they opened the door only in the mornings. On that day, too, Oviya sat on a chair and watched the sleeping Nandhini, feeling something twinge in her mind. She consoled herself that something had happened in her visit to her place. But when Nandhini suffered, unable to open her eyes, she understood everything.

As they were both nurses, they had gotten the vaccine first as frontline workers. Nonetheless, they caught the infection.

Nandhini slowly opened her eyes and heard Oviya calling their hospital to book a home test; she understood everything. Oviya also let the hostel management know that everyone on the second floor should be tested. And as they had expected, they had both tested positive, but thankfully it was a relief that no one else on their floor was affected. After that, they made many arrangements, including bags for food and medicines to be dropped via the hook in their window. All of their friends were ready to help them.

The first two days, no significant effect was visible in their bodies. But on the third day, Nandhini's cough and fever increased, and she could not tolerate it. When there were power outages, they opened the windows to let some fresh air in.

Though Oviya was affected as much as Nandhini, she was eager to help. And whenever Oviya's hands touched her, Nandhini went back to her childhood, vaguely remembering going to bed, hugging her mother.

Nandhini believed that Oviya's caring nature and dedication was in her genes. So far, she has saved three people's lives using CPR. And once, she had done this in front of Nandhini herself. That event happened on a train when they returned from Nandhini's house on a Sunday evening. Though the rail cars were not crowded, the seats were occupied. The couple sitting in front of them would have been about 60. Nandhini indulged in casual conversation with them as Oviya sat, reading a novel. But as the conversation ceased, Oviya looked up and instructed, "Nandhini, quick! Take that bedsheet."

She held up the man who had leaned back with his hand over his chest. He started to lose his heartbeat in seconds. Though Nandhini knew what to do in theory, she gave the highest priority to helping Oviya. Together, they helped the man lay down and then sent his wife away, asking her to help them control the crowd. Oviya began the first aid with CPR. Though she tried hard to press his chest rhythmically and get his breathing back, she was unsuccessful.

"Nandhu, you press his chest twenty times; I'm going to try mouth-to-mouth resuscitation," Oviya said and tried to get him to breathe. And with continuous effort, they got results on the sixth try. He started `breathing again and was coughing. The women felt tears of relief touch their eyes. His wife came along, and in the next station, the train stopped in; the duo sent him off to a hospital and sat back in their seats. Nandhini was very happy and proud about saving someone's life."

"This is enough of a high point in my nursing career," she said.

"This is our duty, Nandhu. We have to save so many lives like this," Oviya replied, gently squeezing her hands.

"How are you taking this so lightly, Oviya?"

"After Cuba, my state remains the one training the most number of nurses in the world. My elder brother supersedes me. He is the kind that will save people by putting his life on the line."

"What is he working as?"

"He is a fireman. He is visiting me next week. I will introduce you both."

After meeting Oviya's brother, Nandhini realized that Oviya had not exaggerated. He had spent just two hours with them, but he introduced a lot of things to Nandhini. For example, he told her that like doctors had to tick a special box in railway reservation forms, fire-fighters also had to tick a special box called 'FF'.

When they were walking close together in the market street, on noting an electric scooter pass by noiselessly, he exclaimed, "Hereafter we have to be very careful while crossing the road. Or we will get into more accidents,"

"I can't understand!"

"Earlier, we could be careful and turn, based on the noise from oncoming motorbikes but now, with these noiseless bikes, we could turn without knowing and that increases the chances of accidents. As scientific improvements happen, humankind's behaviour changes are also essential."

For two days after his departure, Nandhini was constantly thinking about him. But after Oviya informed her that he was engaged and would be married in a few months, Nandhini did not feel much of an attraction. But she felt second-hand pride on knowing that he had saved four people so far from fire accidents.

"What are you deep in thought about?" Oviya asked, turning around in bed.

"I am thinking about you?"

"What about me?" Oviya asked, sitting up.

"Why did you not study to become a doctor?"

"All that is bygone," Oviya said, getting up. "Do you want coffee?"

Nandhini nodded and relapsed into thought. She completed the line of thinking and asked, "Is it impossible to find a medicine for this Corona Virus, Oviya?"

Oviya brought coffee in two glass tumblers, and she handed one to Nandhini and kept the other on the table. She then tied her hair into a bun.

"This is affecting the RNA. That is the issue."

"But nowadays they are solving even genetic issues!"

"They'll formulate a medicine for this too, but it will take time," Oviya said and began drinking her coffee. "I think we will be okay in a couple of days, Nandhu."

"How so?"

"For the last four days, when I wake up from sleep, my body did not support my weight. But now that problem has reduced."

"That means I'll be okay too, right?"

"Let us see. I think your body type would take a few more days to heal. But don't lose courage. When your mind is strong, your healing would be faster."

"When you are with me, why would I worry?" Nandhini rose and came to Oviya, pinching her cheeks.

"Okay, I'm going to use your pads this time," Oviya said softly and went to the bathroom.

"Oh and amidst all the other problems this has to add on too," Nandhini commented and started reading that week's magazine issue. But she was unable to read like before and realised that the effects of this attack would take time to change, and leaned back on the bed. She got worried about the increasing oxygen scarcity in the hospitals. This corona was giving so many issues and troubles. The second dose of vaccine would come in a few days. Maybe the disease's strength would reduce after that. Due to the second wave, people would have better awareness and take their vaccines. Fear of death would make them get vaccinated. She could not understand why so many people were still hesitating.

"Nandhu, shall we play card games?" Oviya asked, coming out of the bathroom.

"Okay, come. Let us pass some time."

They started playing rummy. Nandhini asked, "Are you getting messages from the doctor?"

"A lot of advice, and so much of care as if I am the only one in this world affected by this."

"Why don't you propose directly and marry him?"

"That won't happen, Nandhu. He is like a kid elephant trained with a small rope tied to its legs. Let him break away from that. Then we'll see."

"If it were me, I would have done it long back."

"You don't know about his family. He plays the flute very well. One day, he called me for a function at his place, and that was when he gave me a surprise...."

"What was that?"

"Somehow he learned that my favourite song was 'Ennavo... Ennavo' and he played it before everyone that day, completely flooring me. I was impressed. But when his mother said she was seeking a doctor bride for him, I felt that was the right decision for him."

"Okay, why don't you try dating?"

"He is not such a person... He is still momma's boy."

They continued their conversation as they played. Oviya won the first game, and Nandhini needed just one card to win the second one.

"In just a couple more years, kids will start calling us 'aunty', Oviya," Nandhini said.

"What's wrong with you? You look like an angel, and no one can reject you...."

"I should ask the astrologer; only he knows why. But still, I am not getting your style and poise."

"That will come automatically. You have changed a lot in this one year," Oviya consoled.

"All thanks to you," Nandhini said, recording her first victory. And she also won the third game, so Oviya started playing with more focus.

"Would those who died from Covid get everything done properly, Oviya?"

"Why should we worry about it? But I think the number of people who benefited from this disease's compensation materials would be higher than those who were affected by this."

"I think lady luck favours them now, then," Nandhini said. Oviya won the fourth game, and they realised that the sky was darkening outside.

"Enough of the games," Nandhini said, switching on the lights. They got a call from the hospital.

"Oviya... Your doctor is also affected by covid," Nandhini informed.

Unable to respond, Oviya went and sat on the cot. Her heart was longing to take care of him. She thought he would feel refreshed if she called him. But maybe that would lead to other issues, she thought and calmed herself. It was natural for him to have a doctor wife. And to prevent thinking about him further, she started talking to Nandhini.

"I think we are in for a tough time for the next few years, Nandhu. We will always be busy, and I am not sure how many people will try to sway our hearts," Oviya lamented with pain.

"Yeah. I am afraid too. But I am also feeling a strange hope alongside."

"I think this is going to destroy humanity."

"It won't be that bad, Oviya. They will find a medicine soon."

"But people should understand that. Like how youngsters avoid wearing a helmet, people are not taking this seriously. Then they come to the hospitals, cry there, and make us feel bad. The government is giving us so many directives. If they follow that, they could prevent a lot."

"If those who make the rules flout those themselves, how could we blame the people?" Nandhini said, and Oviya relapsed into silence. She did not speak further but got immersed in her thoughts. Nandhini got a call and said, "Food is coming. Open the window and hang the hook on the other side, Oviya."

They finished the dinner without leftovers. After a while, they had their tablets. Nandhini lay on her cot and started sleeping, while Oviya took her mobile and started reading the messages she had gotten. On seeing Nandhini toss and turn on her bed, Oviya went near her before switching off the lights. Even in this exhausted state, Nandhini's beauty had not diminished. Oviya stood for a few minutes, admiring her beauty. Then she switched off the lights and went to her bed. Why was Nandhini so beautiful nowadays? Oviya wondered. Then she felt a kind of intimate attraction growing inside her. To prevent that, she distracted herself on her mobile.

They recovered in a few days and resumed work. The workload was high, and they had no time to speak like before and were always busy on their feet.

The beds at the hospital were full. And Nandhini could not handle that workload. She felt as if she was in a war field in the middle of a full-on war. Even when she was sleeping at night, she dreamed that she was at work. So, the exhaustion overflowed to the next day too. For the first time, she felt it would be good to hug someone while going to sleep.

And at that midnight hour, Nandhini crawled into Oviya's bed and hugged her close. Though surprised at Nandhini doing this, Oviya embraced her happily.

CHAPTER FIVE

Vicky

Vicky went into extreme distress every time he saw the words RIP on his mobile screen. They scared him all the more when he was isolated in a small room and such news reached him via social media. Earlier, even the occasional bad news affected him, and he felt sad. And when such information came more frequently, he felt himself going mad.

Even if such news was frequent during the first wave of the Covid pandemic, it did not create this harmful an impact. It passed by as bits of information about something distant. But during the second wave, when such news came from his close circle, it made his routine life go awry every day. 2-3 known people died every day, and the RIP messages shattered him completely. Fear rose in him as he wondered if the news would spread the same way when he died. He even got into an argument about this with his boss.

And the boss ordered his employees not to share such news via social media. He added that they could express their grief via company email if necessary. Though this reduced the instances of the word, it was still strong in the status messages. That prompted him to send a message to the group.

'Seeing two-three photos every day with grief-filled RIP messages affects people like me who are in isolation. So please stop from sharing such news for a while.'

Consequently, he got a call from the General Manager within minutes.

"Vicky, dear, no one will stop this for anyone else. You take care of your health. If you want, you can switch off your phone and buy books online so you can sit at home and read."

"I will do that, Sir," said Vicky. But in the next few minutes, he got a call from the Assistant Manager of his department.

"Sir, how are you?"

"I am better now... What's the matter?"

"Sir, since you are not here, a lot of people are not following the rules."

"Why? Only half our people are there per shift. We are running at 50% occupancy, right?"

"Yes sir, but still, about 70-80% people come sometimes."

"You can take action, right?"

"Production is not listening sir. HR is also saying that they will take care. I do not know what to do, Sir."

Unable to answer immediately, Vicky went into thought. If left unchecked, the situation would worsen. Something had to be done. If he was at the office, everyone would listen. But they'd not obey his juniors.

"Sir, are you on the line?"

"Yes, Kumar, Please go to the IT department, and ask them to share the live CCTV feed on my mobile. I will take care of the rest."

It took two days to get that done. That too, when Vicky wrote an angry mail, with their boss in CC. The issue blew up, and he finally got the link.

He could see the live footage of the 24 CCTV cameras in the office on his mobile. It seemed like the company's standards had slipped a bit since the last ten days. The workers had their helmets in their hands as they walked around; things were strewn around on the ground. These and several other unforgiveable safety violations angered him.

Had his absence given them the courage to do such things? Unable to believe the violations, he called the HR manager, detailed the situation, and asked him to take immediate and appropriate action. The HR manager agreed and assured him that the situation will be corrected immediately. But the production manager could easily cast this aside. And to ensure that the production did not dip during these times, his salary bonus would be high. No matter how many times his promotion had been denied due to breaking safety norms, they could not stop his salary hike. Though the people who had joined the company along with him had become general managers, he was still a manager. But the salary remained on par.

This was the state of the country. To change this, multiple waves of the pandemic should come, and only then people will take matters of safety and hygiene more seriously. That too, only for a while. Their routine lifestyle and work would go back to the earlier ways in a few months. If the reasons for this were researched, it would only result in a headache. Vicky decided not to think about those things during his illness and tried to relax. But the situation in the company continued to worry him. Everyone was flouting rules. He had to but a stop to this before things went out of hand.

At that time, the news of a labourer's death spread, and in a few minutes, his photo and a condolence message was uploaded as status by almost everyone in the company. That employee was a person who followed the safety rules carefully. So, Vicky called the production manager to enquire about this. At first, Vicky spoke well, but when it came to the issue of the company's safety, his throat stuck. And that was the undoing. The production manager immediately jumped onto the chance, saying, "Why, sir, why are you straining yourself at this time? You don't bother about this. We will take care. You return safely and then take care of all the safety rules."

"But before I return, it looks like everyone in the company will get Covid..."

"Sir, Covid will not affect anyone working here. Only those whose bodies are weak will be affected. Our employees are strong. Don't worry about all this. We will take care," he said and disconnected the call.

It did not skip Vicky's attention that the man kept saying 'we'.

He sent a carefully worded email about this to all the general managers and focused on his health. Though his temperature was not high like before, the exhaustion affected him.

Amidst all this, he heard that his aunt had died of Covid and Vicky suffered, unable to take the grief. His aunt's death, the laments, and the RIP status messages did not affect him much. His family did not share much of the news with him either. Vicky wondered if his aunt's death had become a piece of ordinary information for him. He could not accept that fact. Had the news of death everywhere changed his heart? He could not think further about it.

In a few days, he felt better, and he came back to work and tried to correct everything. He made the words‘ safety first' become foremost in everyone's minds again. Busy with work, he had forgotten his birthday completely. He woke up in the morning, drank his coffee, worked out for a bit, and then as he was soaping himself during a bath, he remembered his aunt. In his younger days, when his aunt soaped him, he would feel ticklish due to her hands, and she would chase him around to bathe him again. She would call on his birthdays without fail and wish him. "Son, happy birthday to you."

But now, he would not hear her voice anymore. Vicky's heart yearned for her loving blessings, and he crumbled a bit inside. Since her death, the news brought on indescribable pain inside him for the first time. He stood under the shower as, for the first time in his life, his body shook with sobs and copious tears.

CHAPTER SIX

Sangamithirai

The General Manager was watching as Sangamithirai opened the door and exited. He was 52. While restive, he was considering taking voluntary retirement in a few years. He was also thinking of starting a new business from the settlement he would get. Despite all this, the General Manager never lost interest in his current job. Everything had become easier after getting a manager like Sangamithirai. She finished all her work diligently, with intelligence and sharp focus. He had praised her work several times. He was expecting such a woman that would be return to her room within a few minutes of leaving.

He could not dispel the occasional guilt that rose inside him, wondering if he was the reason for everything. He consoled himself that there was only so much he could do as the whole world was suffering. But he had gotten to know within very few days that he had been the spreader of the dreaded virus to the entire office.

In accordance with his designation and wanting to stand as an example, he got himself tested. And until he subjected himself to it, he had no symptoms. But on the way back, he realised that there were some issues with his breathing and eyesight. His driver had even teased him, "What is this, sir? Did you catch it from the hospital?"

By the time he reached home, he felt unusually weak. Even then, he just informed his wife that he would rest for awhile and reclined on the bed. When his wife woke him up for dinner, he realised that his body temperature had risen. Immediately, he instructed his wife and children to keep their distance and isolated himself. His family understood the gravity of the situation and gave their complete cooperation.

Immediately, he also called Sangamithirai and instructed that everyone should get themselves tested. As he had expected, the results turned out positive for him and 20 others in the office. He was amazed that it spread so widely with no symptoms at all.

Luckily, his wife and children had not contracted the virus and he was relieved. His whole office would tease him that like everything else, he was the forerunner in this too! There were no fatalities in the spread of the virus, but the associated fear and guilt shook his core. It could also be said that while the visible effects had passed, there were many invisible effects. An example would be the changes in Sangamithirai's behaviour.

The virus had affected her household, and both husband and wife were affected simultaneously, eventually isolating themselves in rooms on the upper floors of their house. Her poor teenage children had taken care of them and the house without any complaints. In those two weeks of suffering, her respect for and trust in her children had increased manifold. Having behaved like children until then, they had risen to the occasion and proven that they could do everything. Both the children took care of their parents, over days and nights.

Even after the couple had completed their isolation, the children did not allow them to do any work for a while after. In a few days, after Sangamithirai and her husband had fully recovered, they comfortably wore the garb of children again. And Sangamithirai indulged them, not letting them do any more house work. She understood only much later that, although she had recovered from the infection, she could not do her work as before. She consoled herself that it could be because of the increased workload. But she was not convinced or at peace. She could understand that something was wrong. She could not explain what it was, though. She asked her husband if he noticed any differences in her actions, and he responded saying that nothing much had changed and everything was due to the physical strain. Her children did not give her any clear answers either.

It was her General Manager who made her aware of the changes gently, in a subtle way, so that he did not offend her. 'It is nothing big, ma... Nowadays when I dictate something, deviate to a different topic and return to the original subject I was dictating, you are not able to recall and pick up the threads like before. You are forgetting a few things... That's all!' he explained. It was only then that it hit her. She finally understood why her workload was increasing.

'All this confusion would last just a few days, ma. And everything will go back to normal soon. You don't worry yourself much ruminating over this, okay?'

'Sir, how should I manage and overcome this, then?'

'Very simple. Don't feel shy to bring a notebook next time and note down everything I say, understand?'

'Okay, Sir, I will do as you say,' she agreed, and prepared herself for that change in the habit. The General Manager, for his part, split up her workload into manageable segments and did not burden her all at once. She recovered and improved within a few days. And now, when she left his office, she was as confused about the work assigned to her. Remembering only the things he had said a couple of days ago, she panicked and hastened back to his room. Having expected her arrival, he had kept his door open and welcomed her with a smile.

'Sorry, Sir,' she said.

'It's okay, ma. I figured that when you did not bring the notebook, that you may have to come back to verify. Okay, now try to recollect whatever work I assigned to you...'

'Sir... You told me about the vendor problem in that...project...'

'Then?'

'Since the rainy season is approaching, you asked me to arrange for a snake bite precautionary training...' she listed, trying to recollect as much as she could. He was patiently listening to her. Then he said gently, 'You have managed to recollect 90% of what I said. Just 10% more. And even that will be okay in a few days. You may leave now.'

When she returned to her seat, Sangamithirai called her husband with elation.

But her husband wasn't answering her phone. As he was a cashier in a bank so he promptly switches on the mobile button and kept ideal on the desk after few minutes he would answer. This time it was different, she started going into spirals of deep thought.

When she called again after a while, the phone still went unanswered. She understood that something was wrong. She sent a text to him asking him to call her back as soon as he saw it, and began waiting anxiously. "Reduce consequence" she muttered as she looked at the Buddha statue on her desk. She got a call from him in some time.

"There was a small problem, dear. I will explain when you are back home."

"That's okay, please tell me now!"

"Instead of sending 50 lakhs to an account, I sent 5 crores. I have done such a mistake for the first time in life."

"Is the problem sorted now or not?"

"Yes, we corrected that. But first time I feel guilty," he said.

CHAPTER SEVEN

Abhi

Abhimanyu, also known as Abhi, was watching Maari Annan. How many changes were happening with him! He was taking care of all the patients in the Covid ward with extreme care. These were recent changes, in effect only since the last few days. It would be good if this continued even after he went out. There were 16 people in the ward. People from all castes and creeds were together there, and it made Abhi's heart happy. He paused to think about the current changes in society and the change in people's nature.

For the last few years, people were creating gangs based on their caste and forming local mafia gangs, showing an illusion of power in their local areas. They would sit in the public places of their towns during nights and even get drunk sometimes. Though the elders of the town knew this, they hardly protested.

But Abhi knew very well that this would develop into a riot soon. Even in the grocery stores in the city nearby, it had become a habit to ask indirectly, "Which people are you?"

Initially, Abhi did not understand the meaning of that question. It was the shop assistants who explained it to him. "You are growing, right... they are not able to tolerate that," they said.

Since that day, Abhi learned to be careful while talking to anyone. Whenever anyone started conversations about castes and political parties, he would escape from there. But when he saw the same thing happen in his town too, he got the urge to do something about it.

It was a small consolation that this did not spread onto the village sports and games.

"Abhi, come. Let us go and play," said Maari Annan.

Abhi raised his head to look at him, saying, "I need to go to the bathroom. Will come," and moved off.

The bathroom was very clean. In the place of the sterile smell that usually permeated hospitals, there was a pleasant smell nowadays. Every morning and evening, the janitors came in full protective gear and cleaned the areas. It was only now that the full implication of the word 'hygiene' is felt everywhere. If this continued, we could probably get a hygienic lifestyle. But people are not of the nature to change that way! They would look to construct others' lifestyles based on their utilitarian values. No matter how many disasters came, they would be crushed only temporarily and get back on their feet. When the bad calamities came, it was the norm to watch helplessly as they wreaked havoc.

Abhi had believed, a few years ago, that all this would definitely end one day. But that felt like a dream now, as he considered the seriousness of this current situation.

He got a video call from his wife.

"Where are you going?"

"To play volleyball."

"Should you play in your current health situation?"

"How long can I spend lying on the bed? I would feel better once I play for a while."

"Okay... Our daughter wants to speak to you," she said and handed the phone to the girl.

"Dear... How are you?"

"I am good, Daddy... When are you coming home?"

"I will definitely come next week. You be good and safe with Amma..."

"Okay."

"Don't go outside. Or you will catch Covid too. Then you have to be alone like me. Do you understand?"

"Okay, Daddy..."

"And eat well. Only then you won't get covid."

"Okay, Daddy."

"Give the phone to Amma." H spoke to his wife and then walked to the volleyball ground behind the hospital compound. He felt sad when he thought of his wife.

The virus would have spread to his mother, grandmother, mother-in-law and daughter too. But they were not affected by this. When his mother and grandmother were suffering from cough and weakness, he insisted on getting them tested, but they refused. And thanks to them, his wife did not get herself tested either. He had a slight doubt due to this and got himself tested; the result was positive. He realised it was of no use to chastise them and started back to the hospital. In two days, his father followed him and the hospital did not allow any women to visit.

Since it was a developing village, a lot of rumours spread. No outsider was allowed into the village. Even if the people of the village went out and returned, they were quarantined for a few days.

The virus would have spread to everyone at home. But he believed that the women recovered from it faster. It was a bit of a relief to him that the disease did not affect the women of the village whose bodies were strengthened by the village lifestyle. He doubted that men were mistakenly portrayed as the stronger gender.

That evening, he played for two hours, returned to the ward, bathed, and ate his dinner. The lights in the ward would be switched off by 9 PM. Whenever anyone spoke over the phone, it would be heard clearly throughout the room, so no one attended any calls. Even if some older people flouted the rules, the nurses called out from afar and made them sleep.

He would also speak with his family and sleep. Tired out by his playing, he would get good sleep. But around 2 AM, he would wake up. Two other older men would also be lying awake, like him. They would gesture at him, asking, "Are you not able to sleep?"

Then the three of them would go out to the volleyball grounds and sit on the benches there. Since it was summer, the gentle breeze and the darkness of the night would create an understanding. They would sit there, talking until 5 in the morning. Once it struck 5 AM, they would walk around the grounds. Around 6 AM, they would drink their coffees and teas that came to the ward and their day would begin.

Then the older men would finish their breakfast and take a nap. Later, they'd play carrom or spend time scrolling their mobile for news or movies, lying on their beds. Before noon, they would hear the news of someone's death. They would finish lunch while talking about that, then take a nap again. They would talk about how the virus affects other parts of their body. The older men, unable to discuss a lot of things openly, would swallow their troubles.

So far, there was no death in their wards, and this kept giving the occupants hope and energy. They go the medicines and tablets at the right time. They loved the timely action of the new government. Abhi was surprised to note that some were praising the government no matter what political party they were affiliated with. For someone who believed that political parties always operated with a vendetta, this was a new experience.

Getting a negative result for the third time, Abhi returned home. His father returned a few days later. Though they wanted to return to their usual routine, their situations did not cooperate. The government's restrictions continued.

Abhi began spending his days with his daughter. His wife noticed their closeness developing like never before and got worried. Even after the government's restrictions lifted, Abhi had not reopened his shop and was roaming around with his daughter. Though his wife consoled herself saying that this was the effect of that unexpected short separation, she realised that it had been too many days since he had opened his shop, and finally forced him to do that.

He then made it a habit to start later, and returned home earlier to spend time with his daughter. His wife thought long about it and spoke to him one night.

"Look here, I thought you were exceptionally affectionate on our daughter because you were separated for a few days. But it is going beyond limits now. You have to be the firm father as usual. If you shower so much love on her and not even scold her when needed, it would affect only us in future."

"I understand everything, dear. But without my knowledge, something has been changing inside me."

"What are you saying?"

"It was not just those twenty days... Something else is there. That is why my behaviour has also changed..." he said, his confusion apparent.

CHAPTER EIGHT

Dhivya

"Dear, have you taken everything?"

"Yes, Ma."

"Keep an extra mask and your sanitizer handy."

"Okay, Ma."

"I don't have the heart to send you, dear..."

"I don't have the heart to go either, Ma... I feel frail. But students have started coming to the college. I have already taken twenty days of leave. It'll be a problem if I take more."

"There's no problem in that place, right?"

"No, Ma. They've assured us that every room has been sanitised. They're also saying that there are no active cases..."

On hearing the horn of a taxi outside their house, Dhivya opened the window.

"Ma, the taxi has arrived. Inform Rahul and Dad. Let the children be with my husband home's, it is for the best," she said as she took leave of her mother.

Dhivya was carrying a trolley bag and a handbag. She had never before felt her shoulder bag weighing down as it did now. She wondered if she had lost even the strength to drag the trolley bag along.

It was all due to the damned virus. It had affected not just her body but also brought on many invisible side effects. It is saddening that one was unable to do anything to safeguard themselves against the virus! The scientific world suffered from guilt when the infamous Malaysian flight disappeared, and things were following in a similar vein nowadays.

She spoke over a video call with her husband and children during the taxi ride. While she had isolated herself in her parents' house, her children were safe with her husband in the village.

She had to cross two states to join work again. But Dhivya slept through most of her journey before she reached her quarters at 6 in the morning. After a short rest, she felt it would be refreshing to wake up at 8 AM. Her department was just 100 metres away. So she would step out of the house at exactly 08:50 AM. But college timings had changed now.

The new timings were 09:00 AM to 04:00 PM. This was also good for her. She could take more rest and regain her strength and health. So she twisted and turned in her bed, thinking. How beautiful the world had been before everything had turned upside down in just a few days. She had not read of such disastrously painful situations even in fictitious stories. Who could be blamed? And would it all be resolved by blaming someone? Who could be held responsible when there was no evidence? Would it become the norm to live with this given that the virus was mutating? Would human bodies prepare and alter themselves according to that? That could just be possible...

Humankind had evolved to its current state after so many natural calamities. Would this amazing life form—that overcame so many obstacles—be felled by this mere, invisible virus? Never! Such a thing won't happen! We have technologies to prevent asteroids from millions of miles from hitting the earth, and we shall not be defeated by such trivialities. We have just been caught unawares.

Just a few more months. When we retaliate, we would ensure that such a virus strain never exists in this world. We have destroyed so many such microbes that have troubled mankind. We will do the same to this virus, too, in a few days. But how many lives will be lost in the process?! We have suffered the loss of many lives while the evolution from neanderthal to human form happened. Was this a similar thing? Was this not made by nature, though? So it still was a bit debatable. Not many prominent politicians' lives have been lost. Maybe if such a thing happened, the scientific world might find the best cure faster?

Her thoughts ran in all directions. When she took her mobile off the bed and checked the time, it was 08:40 AM. Deciding to get her breakfast from the department canteen, Dhivya made to get up from her bed. But she could not get up quickly like before. Somehow, with a lot of effort, she managed to get up, take a bath, get ready, and walk to the department. Everything looked new, and she felt slightly anxious. She reassured herself that such feelings were common when she returned from vacations at home and walked along.

The entire day went by without the feeling of familiarity that she usually had. Her students were the same batch from the previous semester. But she felt there was a chasm in between. She could not process what it was. She could see herself struggling to take classes with her earlier efficiency, but managed it well with her experience. The guilt remained, though. She hoped that things would go back to normal in two or three days. The workday came to an end before she could ruminate further on the issues.

Her lunch from the mess in the afternoon had seemingly upset her stomach, so she returned to her quarters and fell asleep. She woke up around 08:00 PM and thought of getting her dinner from the mess. But she felt that if her neighbours saw her, she would be teased. 'Could a woman not cook even for herself?' they'd remark. So she made herself some *upma*, had it, spoke to her husband and children via a video call again and took her tablets just as sleep started to caress her eyes.

When she woke the next morning, though her body felt refreshed, her mind felt as if she had returned from her leave only that day. The thought followed her all day and she could not understand why.

She avoided thinking about it, reassuring herself that it would be sorted in a couple of days. But despite a week going by, the same thought assaulted her every morning. Was her heart still not getting accustomed to this place? She found the entire experience nag her mind. When the same feeling lasted for a few more weeks, she realised that something was wrong with her. She also understood that this could not be cured just with tablets. She wondered if she was exhibiting symptoms of depression. She avoided being alone assuming that would lead her to take some bad decisions. She ensured that someone was near her at all times. And she began spending more time over the phone.

"What is this, dear? Nowadays you are calling me a lot... Are you afraid? Better take leave and come home. You can take your classes online," her husband suggested.

She applied for leave and the management approved it without any hassle.

Dhivya's life returned to her normal routine with her husband and children. Even though she stumbled a bit with the online classes, her students cooperated well.

Eventually, she felt it was enough. It did not feel right to continue this way. So, she went back to the college again.

As someone who usually fell into a routine in a few days, she did not suffer like earlier and got into the groove on the sixth day. That morning, she felt as if she had been reborn. As she was combing her hair, she heard the doorbell. There was no one outside when she opened the door. But when she peeped out, she could see Rashid walking away. Deep in thought, she walked back into her room. The same thing had happened the night before. Why? Why was he behaving like that?

He lived in the same building, a floor above her, with his wife. He had never spoken a word to her. So he probably had rung her doorbell by mistake, she convinced herself.

But the interesting thing was that she did not know that he had also suffered the deadly virus and had come out of the ordeal.

CHAPTER NINE

Dimple

It is not sure how the teacher found it out on the tenth day of us reaching the tenth standard. But as if she realised that Sangeetha and I were communicating with our eyes, she said, "Dimple and Sangeetha, don't talk to each other."

For all that mattered, she was drawing something related to the environment on the blackboard. I was amazed by how she had found out.

Earlier, when we used to talk to each other in whispers, the male teachers either did not realise or did not bother. But no matter how low our voices were, female teachers found out and punished us. We were on the fourth bench then. But nowadays, due to social distancing norms, I was forced to sit on the sixth bench, that too alone. How can we whisper to each other in this situation? And masks were mandatory too. We would get scolded for flouting the rules. The school management has given us masks to wear. Maybe in a few days, the masks would be branded with the name and logo of the school!

Since recent reasonably, we can understand even if we talk on masks. I have to say that the eyes are a reason too, and it is far easy to understand the emotions expressed by the eyes.

Nowadays, my communication with Sangeetha is not just with words. We are speaking clearly just with our eyes. Was this a prize from Corona? I do not know. Because, earlier, to express our thoughts, we had to use our hand gestures and then speech. But women's emotional quotient is slightly higher. When girl students reach out to female teachers to complain about something, they understand the issue from a distance just with the expressions. Poor male teachers, though! They know only after a detailed, wordy explanation. Was this because women are more sensitive? Though they understand so many things quickly, why do they falter in mathematics? That is a mystery.

If someone could talk about this, it would be the lecturer in the opposite house. I have not spoken much to him, maybe four times in the last two years. Last week, I had to talk to him because we were confined in a lift.

When we were going up in the lift, there was a power failure, and we got an opportunity to talk for ten minutes. He asked about what I was studying and my name. Then he asked for the meaning of my name, and I replied, "It means, 'believe in yourself."

"Then how do we call you?"

"Call me Dimple. That is my nickname," I replied.

The talk then drifted to the second wave of Covid. I spoke about the changes happening in my school. He said about the changes that people around us were going through. Meanwhile, the security guard came to the floor above, stood near the door of the lift and said, "Sir! This was repaired only yesterday, and the mechanic has said he'd come only by tomorrow. Sorry Sir, the power will be restored soon."

"Okay, you go. I will take care," he said.

Then I spoke to him about my talent in astrophysics. When we talked about time, he asked, "Have you found out the time?"

"No," I replied.

Then he explained about the universe and how fast it was expanding. After that, he asked, "Okay, it is getting late. Shall we escape from this?"

"There's no electric power, though," I pointed out.

"Watch this," he said, opening the grill of the lift. When he kicked the outer door, it moved but did not open. He called me closer and pointed out a wheel between the building and the lift. He told me that the lift would open if we pulled it and did that while asking me to push it towards the door. When I put my strength on it, the door opened quickly.

"It is a wonderful technique!" I said happily.

"I have many more such escaping techniques," he said, laughing. I reached my floor even as we continued talking. My mom came out to see who I was talking to and went back in.

Our conversations went on to include more exciting topics. He absolutely refused to accept the possibility of teleportation, which was one of my favourite topics. He kept stacking arguments against it. And in the end, I responded that, though it was not scientifically probable, it was one of my favourite troops.

"This is the weakness of this generation," he commented. Not to be outdone, I pointed out the achievements of this generation but also accepted the fact that we feel like wasted youth outré by the wilder talks.

Then he asked if we were going in the right dimension. He observed that it had become necessary for us to talk to communicate our thoughts. I spoke about how Sangeetha and I communicate with our eyes. Then he said that parents find out what had happened to their children by their mere gestures. So, it was even more critical, especially in these Covid times, to check which dimension we are travelling in.

"This virus has decimated lakhs of lives from the face of this Earth. Imagine how it would be if it were crores! Just the people of your generation would remain. Even that is not a certainty. Because the virus would have mutated and could even destroy the younger generation!"

When he realised that I was listening to everything attentively, he continued happily. He briefed that by understanding the concepts like telepathy completely and reaching a different dimension, we could communicate with other life forms. Though such ideas were new to me, I have seen my mother and her brother speak to each other with just willful thought. My father used to say, "Even if I have to hit you jokingly, I have to ask your brother's permission, or we'll immediately get a call."

The lecturer also detailed things based on my interest in astrophysics.

"Now you are amazed by the universe, you are eager to see what is in it. Soon, your interest will go to a different level, and then you will want to go to space to see what is there. So prepare yourself accordingly."

That was when I realized the extent of my dreams.

"When I first saw you two years ago, I was wondering what this girl was doing here. Now I understand."

"What did you think when you saw me?" I asked eagerly.

He paused a little and said softly, "You are the next Kalpana."

CHAPTER TEN

Anu

Nalini was surprised that Anu Akka had not attended her phonecalls even after many attempts. She was not of the nature to keep talking to people over the phone, and she used rings only when there was a need. But Anu Akka was not the type to stay quiet either. She would talk over the phone at least fifteen times a day. She would suffer from sleeplessness if she could not do that. By all means, she would speak to the four closest people in her life. If not, she would feel as if she had lost something. She always insisted that there was so much happiness in talking.

Wasn't talking the easy way to express one's emotions and thoughts clearly to others? Who does not get enamoured by words? Of all the life forms in this world, only humankind can talk. Many empires have stood by the power of words, and many love stories have succeeded with talks. And a lot of love stories have failed because people have not spoken at the right time. So much happiness lurks in talking. A toddler's babble creates delight in the heart. No other human feeling matches the exhilaration arising out of it. Only those who do not realise this exists as useless burdens on this Earth.

Though many people called Anu Akka a motormouth, she did not bother. Some even called her 'Akasha Vani', after the popular radio channel, but she was not affected by that either. She always talked nonstop. Even while asleep, she dreamed of talking to her loved ones. Or she would dream of flying to faraway places. Often, she had felt that Lord Vinayagar had crawled along. The following day she would wake and try to recollect what she spoke with Him. She had never realised the truth until then, though.

But nowadays, Anu Akka was behaving as if all this was a thing of the past. Nalini wondered if she spoke a lot to determine the certainty of her existence after the loss of her husband.

The phone near Nalini rang, and Anu akka's name flashed on the screen. Immediately, she attended the call and spoke, "What, akka! You seem to be so busy these days! What, are you holding fort anywhere?"

"Nothing like that, dear," said Anu Akka.

"Then why aren't you answering your phone?"

"I am perusing your horoscope now...."

"Don't you have any other work to do?"

"In just 40 days, someone from the north is arriving to seek you as their bride. You just wait and see!"

"Why? Don't you want me to be peaceful?"

"You are getting older... Is a job enough? Should you not get married on time too?"

"See here. We'll be working from home for some more time. In this situation, I cannot even think of marriage. Please take your astrology and predictions elsewhere."

"All this is science... You won't understand the importance of this now! Okay, will talk to you later," Anu Akka said and cut the call.

Nalini did not know how Anu Akka had gotten interested in astrology. Perhaps she had gotten interested in this to divert herself during free time. Her inclination to keep herself occupied had drawn her into this. Without knowing who to take as her guru in that male-dominated field, she had chosen to learn everything from scratch using videos off YouTube. She also bought the books they suggested and started reading them. Her parents did not oppose this much, either. She insisted that everyone's life existed inside the 330 dimensions whenever she spoke to Nalini, save a few deviations. No one can act beyond it."

She would also add a lot of information regarding that.

Even though Nalini did not find this information helpful, she was interested in what Anu Akka had to say. So, she never stopped her from speaking.

Once, while talking to Anu Akka, Nalini had asked, "Would astrology be fit only for humans or all life forms on Earth?"

"It is for all lives on Earth, Nalini. You just give me the exact time of birth, and I will predict the horoscope correctly," Anu Akka answered carefully.

Nalini gave Anu Akka the exact birth coordinates of a recently birthed calf to suit that need.

"Akka, a child was born in this time. My friend's sister's baby. You should check the horoscope of this child!" Nalini said and even gave a week. Though she spoke with Anu Akka many times after that, she did not bring this up. When she asked about it exactly a week later, Anu Akka asked, "This is a girl child, right?"

"Akka, you are correct!" Nalini exclaimed.

"She will get no support from her father's house. Everything comes from her mother's side."

"Then?"

"Her horoscope looks good. But we should not seek all details now. She will go to a good place only. Let us see the remaining details after she reaches puberty," Anu Akka said.

Laughing, Nalini confessed, "Akka, let me tell you the truth. The details I gave are for the calf that our cow Lakshmi birthed."

Abruptly, Anu Akka cut the call and then did not contact Nalini for more than a month. Though Nalini went to her in person and apologised, Anu Akka spoke harshly. "You are free to speak whatever you want about me; you have all rights to do that. But you have no leeway to speak about my astrology."

Angered by that, Nalini returned home.

Curious to know what was so special about astrology, Nalini checked YouTube for videos of astrologers speaking. She understood one thing. It was not easy to learn this craft, and it would take at least seven years of unwavering dedication even to touch the surface. All these things would not be possible for Anu Akka. She did not have the patience to learn this in-depth. She was probably just enamoured by the glitz of astrology. When Nalini shared her understanding bit by bit, Anu Akka was also alleviated.

But Nalini had never asked what astrology had predicted about the deadly virus. Because this trying period had thrown light on many uncomfortable truths for the world to see, maybe that was why Anu akka—the person who kept talking nonstop about random things to anyone who would listen—nowadays finished her conversations in a few minutes. She even went silent as if there was nothing more to about talk.

Wanting to talk about this primarily, Nalini phoned Anu Akka one day. After all, if the virus had brought about this change, this was a dangerous sign. Likewise, it could have created different side effects with various people.

"What is it, dear? Say! You have called me and are now silent!"

"Akka, you're free now, right?"

"Yeah, what is the matter?"

"No... Nowadays you are not talking to me for more than five minutes. I wondered if...maybe...it was because of the pandemic..." Nalini replied hesitantly.

And for the first time in her memory, Anu Akka responded with a long silence.

About Author

Originally named V. A. Jagadalapradapan, J K Pradap hails from Thandarampattu in Tiruvannamalai district. He finished his schooling in Sathanur Dam, Sathanur, and Thandarampattu. He finished his B.E., (Mech) undergraduatestudies in SVNIT, Surat. He then completed his M. Tech (Industrial Safety Engg) in NIT, Trichy.

He was christened J K Pradap by writer G. Murugan, who also published Pradap's first short story 'Irai' in his magazine named 'Vanam'. His subsequent short stories have appeared in magazines including 'Vanam', 'Manal Veedu', 'NaangaamPaadhai', 'Pavalakkodi'.

His first short story collection based on the post-covid struggles, titled 'Sangamiththirai' was translated and published as an E-Book in March 2022. The original Tamil stories are coming out as 'Sangamiththirai' soon, and the stories that have been published in other stories would be collected and published as 'Vellam', soon.

And following that, Nathikarai Vasam(Tamil Novel) English translation, titled 'Always with you' will also be published, followed by the English translation of the stories in 'Vellam'.

www.ingramcontent.com/pod-product-compliance
Lightning Source LLC
LaVergne TN
LVHW101617210926
848480LV00009B/789